Anita

Anita

Anita Gitts

Mister Penny's Circus

Also by Marie Hall Ets

Mister Penny

The Story of a Baby

In the Forest

Oley: The Sea Monster

Little Old Automobile

Mr. T. W. Anthony Woo

Another Day

Play with Me

Mister Penny's Race Horse

Cow's Party

Automobiles for Mice

Just Me

By Marie Hall Ets and Aurora Labastida

Nine Days to Christmas

Mister Penny's Circus

BY MARIE HALL ETS

NEW YORK · THE VIKING PRESS

Acknowledgment

In making this book I am deeply indebted to the State Historical Society of Wisconsin. At their "Circus Museum," set up on old circus grounds in Baraboo, I was able to sketch actual old tents, ticket wagons, and so forth. But I received even more help from their extensive files of circus material in the Madison Museum and am most grateful to the friendly staff members there.   M.H.E.

MISTER PENNY'S other animals were asleep for the night, but not Splop the goat. Splop had heard strange animal-talk and was sneaking down the road to find out what it was. When she reached the big tree she hid behind the bushes and looked up. 7

What she saw made her race home, wake up all the other animals, and bring *them* back to look too. But neither Limpy the horse, nor Mooloo the cow, nor Pugwug the pig, nor Mimkin the lamb, nor Chukluk the hen, nor Doody the rooster had ever heard or seen animals like the ones in the tree.

"What are they?" asked Splop. "Where did they come from? And why are they wearing clothes? And why all the growling and chattering?"

"I don't know," said Limpy. "But they look friendly. Let's ask them." And he lifted his head and whinnied.

The animals in the tree stopped talking and looked down.

"Excuse me," said Limpy politely. "But do you mind telling us who you are and where you come from?"

"Not at all," said the one with the dress on. "This big fellow with me is Olaf, the bear. And I'm Susie, the chimpanzee. We belong to the circus. We were just doing our tricks in tonight's show when that big storm came and blew the tent down. So we ran away. But now that we are here we don't know what to do. We have no place to sleep and no one to feed us."

"Then why don't you go back?" asked Splop.

"We don't want to," said the chimpanzee. (The bear growled.) "It's fun doing tricks in the shows. But it's no fun being locked up in cages all the rest of the time. And it's no fun being shut in an empty old factory in winter. That's why we ran away when we had the chance."

"Mister Penny will know what to do," said Limpy. "Come home with us and we'll wake up Mister Penny."

But they didn't have to wake up Mister Penny. He had heard Limpy whinny and had come out with his lantern to look around. He had just discovered that all his animals were gone, when in through the gate they came, led by the bear and the chimpanzee.

"My eyes!" he said to himself. "I must be dreaming!" And he held his lantern higher. But then the bear and the chimpanzee came forward and held out their hands like people. So Mister Penny shook hands with them as if they were. And in that way he knew they were real.

"Welcome friends," he said. "Welcome to our house."

"But where under the sun did they come from?" he asked himself. "There have never been any bears or monkeys in this part of the country before." Then he remembered the circus posters he had seen on the barns near Wuddle.

"Oh, that's it!" he said out loud. "You're from the circus! You've run away from the circus! Well, I don't blame you! It's wonderful to be able to do tricks and show people how smart you are. But those cages you have to live in! I wish I could keep you. But I'd have to buy you first and I have no money."

Then he had an idea. "Unless," he said, "unless they'd let me buy you *on time!* Maybe they'll let me buy you *on time* — a little

12

each week! I'll gladly go back to work in the factory to earn the money. But come in! Come in! You must be hungry and tired. I'll fix you some supper and a place to sleep. Tomorrow we'll find the circus and your owners."

The next morning, before the sun peeked over the hill, Mister Penny was up milking Mooloo and making breakfast for the animals. That done, he hitched Limpy to the old cart he had borrowed for the fair. His own animals all gathered around, eager to go to the circus. But Olaf and Susie ran and hid.

When Mister Penny went to get them they threw their arms around

him to show him that they didn't want to go back to the circus — that they wanted to stay with him.

"I'm sorry," Mister Penny said. "I know you don't want to go, and I don't want to take you. But I can't keep you until you are mine. Be so good as to come with me now and I will try my best to buy you. Then I can keep you."

Mister Penny and his family with the two runaway animals reached
the circus grounds just as the parade was returning. So Mister Penny

the people who were crowding around to watch the bear and the chimp-anzee.

"Probably over in the Big Top," they told him. "It's about time for the afternoon show to be starting."

So Mister Penny went on to the biggest tent and asked the man in the ticket wagon where to find the owner.

"The big boss is inside," said the ticket man. "But you can't take your animals in there. *No animals are allowed.*"

Now when Splop heard *that*, she started sneaking away from Mister

Penny. Then, when he wasn't looking, she made a dash for the side of the tent and crawled under. But no sooner was she in than a guard, who thought she belonged to the circus, took her out back and put her in the goat pen. Mister Penny was too busy to notice that she was gone, for the trainer of Susie and Olaf had spied them and came running over to get

them. "Where did you find them?" he asked Mister Penny. "Where were they?" And he reached out his hand to the chimpanzee.

But neither Susie nor Olaf wanted to leave Mister Penny. They pushed closer to him and tried to hide behind him.

"*I* didn't find *them*," Mister Penny said. "*They* found *me*. They came

22

to my house in the night. I figured they belonged to the circus, so I brought them back. But they didn't want to come and I didn't like to make them. I promised I'd try to buy them. But I haven't any money. I'd have to go back to work in the factory and earn the money little by little. Please would it be possible—will you let me buy them *on time?*"

"Well, I'm not the owner," said the trainer. "But I don't think you can buy them *on time*. Trained animals like these are worth too much money."

The trainer could see how much Olaf and Susie wanted to stay with Mister Penny and how much Mister Penny hated to leave them. And that gave him an idea.

"By golly!" he said. "Do you have a good place to keep them? Maybe—if you have a good place to keep them—they could stay with you for the winter. They hate their winter quarters in that empty old factory in Galoopsha. And I don't blame them! Wait here in the big tent after the show and we'll ask the boss."

And as the trainer rushed off with Olaf and Susie he called to the guards at the gate to let Mister Penny and all his animals in.

"And without tickets!" he added. "I want them to see Olaf and Susie perform."

A band was playing and ten beautiful horses were standing up danc-
ing, keeping time to the music, as Mister Penny and his animals took their

26

seats at the side. *I could do that too*, thought Limpy, *if I had the chance. I'm going to try it when I get home!* But while Limpy liked the horses

best and watched all that they did, Pugwug liked the pigs—especially the
ones who could climb a ladder and jump through a hoop.

28

And Mooloo liked the cows and bulls—especially the ones who could seesaw and stand up on platforms.

Mimkin liked the sheep and lambs. *I'd like to jump a fence and go through a hoop like that, too,* she thought.

And Chukluk and Doody liked the chickens. *But that hen isn't lay-ing all those eggs,* thought Chukluk. *It's just a trick.*

Then the center ring was cleared again and a herd of goats came running in—Splop with the others. *That clown, the trainer, will never know*

I don't belong here, Splop thought, *if I just act like the others*. And she gave him a butt from behind.

When the others started climbing to a tightrope high up in the air, Splop tried to follow. But she slid and slipped on the rope ladder and was soon far behind. And when she did reach the top and stepped out onto the tightrope all her feet slipped off at once and she was left hanging.

"Help!" she bleated. "Help! Help!"

The audience thought this was part of a clown act and started to laugh. But not Mister Penny. Mister Penny looked quickly along the row of animals behind him. The next minute he was running out across the sawdust floor and into the ring.

"Hold on!" he called up to Splop. "Just hold on!"

"Oh, please!" he said to the clown, who now saw for himself that the goat was not one of his. "Please get her! Quick, before she falls!"

So the clown slithered up the rope ladder and brought Splop down on his shoulder. Then he spanked her behind and gave her to Mister Penny.

"Oh, thank you! Thank you!" stammered Mister Penny. "I don't know how she . . . I'm sorry! I—"

"Sorry, nothing!" said the clown, under his breath. "It was a good act! Listen to the people laugh!" And he slapped Mister Penny on the back and gave him and his goat a push out of the ring.

But the act had been no joke for Splop. When she got to the seat with Mister Penny she just sat down and hung her head.

"You needn't feel ashamed," Mister Penny told her. "No goat in

the world could do such a trick without a lot of training and practice."

But Splop wouldn't even look up to watch the rest of the show until Olaf and Susie came riding out on their bicycles.

After the show the trainer of Olaf and Susie came and took Mister

Penny to the Menagerie Tent to meet the owner of the circus.

The owner was waiting by the cages of Susie and Olaf. He watched while the trainer undressed them and locked them in. Then he came and shook hands with Mister Penny.

"Thank you, my friend," he said. "Thank you for bringing them safely back. You have earned the reward, and here it is." And he held out five five-dollar bills.

Twenty-five dollars! thought Mister Penny. *Surely* with twenty-five dollars as a first payment the owner would let him buy Olaf and Susie.

"Oh, sir," he said. "Will you keep this twenty-five dollars as a first payment and let me buy Olaf and Susie *on time?* I will go back to work in the factory and earn the rest as fast as I can."

"I'm afraid not," said the owner. "Trained animals like these are worth too much. But the trainer here thinks they would be happier with you for the winter than locked up in the old factory. Do you think you could fix up a proper place to keep them by the time the circus closes in two weeks?"

Oh, sir," said Mister Penny. "I'm sure I can. With twenty-five dollars I can fix up whatever is needed. But I've never kept a bear and a chimpanzee before. I need instructions."

So the trainer started telling Mister Penny what to do to prepare for Olaf and Susie. And while he talked Limpy and Mooloo and

40

Splop and Pugwug and Mimkin and Chukluk and Doody went around the tent looking at all the queer animals. By the time Mister Penny's family started for home even Splop was happy again. They were all thinking what

42

fun it would be to have Susie and Olaf spend the winter with them. And
what fun it would be to try to do all the tricks they had seen at the circus.
During the next two weeks Mister Penny was busy getting ready. He

even made a court in front of the house for bicycle riding. There wasn't time to build new stalls on his long pink house. But he put coops in his own room for Mimkin and the chickens and fixed up their stalls for Susie

44

and Olaf. So when the trainer arrived, he was happy to leave Susie and
Olaf with Mister Penny. And Susie and Olaf were so happy to be with
Mister Penny that they almost hugged the breath out of him.

45

The next day Mister Penny went back to work in the safety-pin factory. "For if I can earn and save enough money," he told the animals, "maybe some day I can buy Susie and Olaf. Then they'll belong in the family and won't ever have to go back to their cages in the circus."

46

And as soon as he was gone Susie started teaching the other animals how to do the tricks they wanted to learn. She made them do easy things first—just as the trainers did in the circus. Then she made them practice and practice until they could do better.

She taught Limpy to run around a track inside the fence at such an even trot that she could jump up and turn a somersault in the air and land on his back again while riding, as she had done with the circus horses.

She taught the chickens to hop like kangaroos. And she taught Pugwug to play *horse*, carrying her on his back like the pig and the clown in the circus.

She taught Mooloo the cow to dance with Olaf the bear while she, Susie, played the horn and kept time.

She taught Limpy to stand on his hind legs while she held a make-believe whip and his reins.

And Susie herself, just from watching Mister Penny, learned the greatest trick of her life. She learned to milk Mooloo. Then Olaf learned

a new trick, too. He learned to balance things on his nose, using pails or anything he could find.

When Mister Penny saw how well his animals were learning their tricks, he began making or buying all the things they needed or wanted. He put up two posts in the garden, with little steps nailed on, and stretched a tightrope between for Splop the goat to walk on. He bought a real circus ball for Olaf to balance and stand on. He painted a hoop for Mimkin to jump through. He bought a ladder for Pugwug, and made a seesaw for Mooloo and Olaf. He bought a clown suit for each of the chickens, and some china eggs for Chukluk the hen to pretend to be laying.

For Limpy he bought a beautiful pink plume.
And he bought him some gold trappings, too.
    And for Susie he bought warm winter under-
wear so she could stay outside in cold weather without catching cold.

But all these things the animals needed or wanted for their tricks took more money than Mister Penny could earn in the factory. (And he wasn't able to save anything toward buying Olaf and Susie from the circus so they wouldn't have to go back to their cages.) He didn't know what to do!

Finally he had an idea. Maybe all the people and their children who came every day to watch the animals perform would help with their pennies. Even the children had pennies. So he painted a big sign on the roof of his house. The sign said:

MISTER PENNY'S 2-PENNY CIRCUS

Then he made another sign with a money box underneath and put this one outside the fence. And when the people read the signs they said, "Yes, of course! A circus costs a great deal of money." And they started dropping all the pennies they had into the box to help buy the things the animals needed or wanted for their tricks.

MISTER PENNY'S
2-PENNY
CIRCUS

PAY
HERE

Before winter was over Mister Penny's animals could do their

tricks as well as any of the animals they had seen in the circus.

Now when the director of the County Fair heard about Mister Penny's circus he came to see it.

"Old man," he said, slapping Mister Penny on the back, "just bring your whole Two-Penny Circus to our fair and we'll have the biggest little fair in the whole country!"

"Oh, sir, I wish I could!" said Mister Penny. "But I can't. The bear and the chimpanzee are not mine and I haven't enough money to buy them. They will have to go back to the big circus and to their cages for summer."

"Well, it would be worth enough to our fair to pay a lot for them," said the director. "Tell me where to find the owner and I'll go see him. And if we can buy them they will be yours to keep. You only have to agree to bring all your animals to the fair grounds each summer during fair week and have them do their tricks."

So the director and his committee went to Galoopsha and saw the owner of Susie and Olaf. And when the owner heard how much they were willing to pay he said yes. He said, "With that much money I can buy a new bear and chimpanzee and have them trained. And in addition I can buy an old elephant that the circus men in Baraboo want to sell me."

60

So Susie and Olaf became part of Mister Penny's family. And the fair director was right. More people came to the fair to see MISTER PENNY'S

2-PENNY CIRCUS than had ever come to any other little fair in the whole country.

And again Mister Penny could just stay home with his family and work in his garden. And he and his family were happier than they had ever been in their lives before, for now Susie and Olaf belonged with them too.

Anita Gritts